Chase's SUPER Sniffer!

Illustrated by MJ Illustrations

Random House New York

 Published in the United States by Random House Children's Books, a division of Penguin Random House LLC, 1745 Broadway, New York, NY 10019, and in Canada by Penguin Random House Canada Limited, Toronto.

randomhousekids.com

ISBN 978-0-399-55373-8

MANUFACTURED IN CHINA

10 9 8 7 6 5 4 3

Chase's super sniffer is always on the case, searching for new scents and awesome adventures.

03

Chase and Marshall are happy to help Farmer Yumi—especially when her apples smell so delicious!

The pups deliver the fresh-picked fruits to Mr. Porter's store. Chase loves the smell of yummy cherries.

Just as they are about to leave, Mandy the monkey escapes from a train that was taking her home to the jungle. She wants Mr. Porter's fruit!

Mandy grabs a bunch of bananas
and flees through a grassy park.

"We have to get Mandy back to her train," Ryder says.

Chase's super sniffer is on the case!

Mandy's trail leads to Katie's pet clinic. Mandy isn't there, but Rubble is. He loves bubble baths.

Next, Chase follows the trail to the beach.
"Have you seen Mandy the Monkey?" he asks.

"She went that way," Zuma barks from the salty sea.

Rocky is busy recycling old tires when Mandy comes running. She jumps and swings through the tires and keeps going.

"Stop that monkey!" Chase barks.

From high in the air, Skye calls Ryder. "I've found Mandy. She's in the pine trees near the Lookout."

Ryder and Chase race to the trees and find Mandy. She is out of bananas, which gives Chase an idea.

Ryder and Chase make a trail of bananas that leads to Mandy's train. Mandy follows the trail to her car and finds . . . a pile of bananas! She is happy to be back.

As the train rolls away, Ryder and the pups wave. "Bye, Mandy!" they say. "Get home safe!"

It has been a busy day for the PAW Patrol—especially for Chase and his super sniffer. Time for a treat!